pK 2617709

PIRATE PRINCESS

More adventures of the

PIRATE PRINCESS

Portia

Coming soon

Pancake

PIRATE PRINCESS

PANDORA

JUDY BROWN

SIMON AND SCHUSTER

For Leo

SIMON AND SCHUSTER
First published in Great Britain by Simon & Schuster UK Ltd, 2006
A CBS COMPANY

3 5 7 9 10 8 6 4 2

Simon & Schuster UK Ltd
Africa House
64-78 Kingsway
London WC2B 6AH

A CIP catalogue record for this book is available from the British Library

ISBN 1 416 90191 4
EAN 9781416901914
Typeset by Ana Molina
Printed and bound in Great Britain by Cox & Wyman Ltd, Reading, Berkshire

Contents

King Brian and Queen Selena

cordially invite you to

the marriage of their daughter

Princess Pandora

to

Prince Norman of Moronia

at 4p.m. in the Royal Chapel

R.S.V.P.

Chapter One

Portia the Pirate Princess leant back in her chair in the Captain's cabin of the *Flying Pig*, and rested her feet on her desk. Portia had been sailing her pirate ship ever since she ran away to sea with her ladies-in-waiting.

Her father, King Bernard, had planned that she would marry the ghastly Prince Rupert, so the very next day she sold her crown to buy the *Flying Pig* and sailed away forever. Jim, the cabin boy of the ship, had stayed on board with Portia and the ladies and become her First Mate.

'One, two, stretch, two . . .' chanted a voice from the main deck.

Princess Peppermint, Portia's cousin, was giving her weekly aerobics class to the ship's crew.

Portia had rescued Peppermint from a fate similar to her own and now Peppermint was the ship's Fitness Officer and a valuable member of the crew.

'Come on, shipmates!' urged Peppermint, 'Put some heave ho into it! Let's see you stretch those muscles. Keep going, Donnatella.'

'Morning, Jim,' said Portia as he walked in with her breakfast tray closely followed by Twiggy, the ship's cat, on the hunt for scraps as usual.

'What delights has Nancy cooked for us this morning?'

Portia studied the plate of food in front of her. It looked a bit like scrambled eggs on toast except that the scrambled eggs were a nasty brown colour and the toast was burnt around the edges, but soggy in the middle.

'How *does* she do that?' thought Portia.

'I'm not sure that I'm that hungry after all, Jim,' she said, poking at the unappealing plate of food with her fork. Twiggy licked her catty lips.

'It does taste a *little* better than it looks,' said Jim helpfully, 'but I could bring you a bowl of porridge if you'd prefer.'

'Hmmm. Porridge would be lovely, thank you, Jim. I thought I could smell cakes a while ago,' said Portia.

'Yes! Nancy's trying to teach herself how to make rock cakes, but I think they're more rock than cake so far. She's on her fourth batch already.'

Portia winced.

'Parrot ahoy!' called Emily, the ship's lookout, from the crow's nest.

Portia walked out of her cabin to meet her parrot, Squawk. She and Peppermint had been putting regular adverts in the 'Princess Daily News' so that any other Princesses in trouble could ask for their help, and Squawk was on his way back with the latest reply.

'Parrot post! Parrot post!' squawked Squawk as he landed on Portia's shoulder.

'What have you got for me today, Squawk?'

She took a piece of paper from Squawk's claw and unrolled it.

'Who's it from?' asked Peppermint, running over to join her cousin.

As Portia began to read the note her face filled with dread. She read the note out loud.

Dear Portia,

I hope you remember me. My name is Princess Pandora of Patagonia, we were in the same year at Princess school and I desperately need your help.

My Uncle Griswald has told me I have to marry Prince Norman of Moronia.

In his country girls are only permitted to cook, sew and knit and do all the other boring girly stuff. I won't be allowed to carry on with my experiments and it's against their law for girls to even use a screwdriver in case they break a fingernail. They've already told me I have to leave my workshop behind and I'm not allowed to carry on with my inventions!

PLEASE, PLEASE, help me. They've put me in the tallest tower in the palace, there are bars on the window and guards at the door. The wedding preparations have already started! Time is running out!

Yours, in desperation.

Princess Pandora

'Oh no!' said Peppermint, 'This is terrible! I remember Pandora, she was always thinking up amazing ideas for gadgets at school. Do you remember the Automatic Bedmaker she invented so that we didn't have to make our beds every morning?'

'Do I?!' exclaimed Portia. 'It was brilliant. Just think how many more incredible things she could come up with. It would be a crime if she had to go and live in such a dreadful place but I don't know if we can get there in time. Jim, let's go and check the charts. Attention shipmates!' she announced. 'Peppermint and Anisha, weigh anchor. The rest of you hoist the main sails. We've got a race on our hands!'

Chapter Two

Portia and Jim looked at the charts and plotted their course.

'I reckon we should just about make it,' said Jim, 'but it'll be a push. I'll go on deck and take the wheel.'

'The question is what to do when we get there though,' said Portia. 'I've never been to Princess Pandora's palace, but if she's in the tallest tower with bars on the window and guards outside, it sounds like it's going to be tricky.'

'You'll think of something, Captain,' Jim said encouragingly as he dashed out of the cabin.

Portia took down a book from the shelf.

'This might help a bit,' she said to herself. It was *The Illustrated A-Z of Palaces and Castles.* 'At least I can have a look at where we're going.'

She turned the pages until she reached a picture of Pandora's palace and studied it carefully.

Peppermint came in and looked over her shoulder.

'As far as I can remember,' said Peppermint, 'the castle is on top of a hill that overlooks the harbour.'

'Yes,' agreed Portia, 'it says here that there's a wall all around it. It's not going to be easy to get in or out.' Portia and Pandora looked at each other. 'This is going to be really tough.'

Meanwhile, in the tallest tower of the walled Palace on top of the hill, Princess Pandora was getting worried. She looked out to sea through the bars on the window with her telescopic viewing device (or TVD as she preferred to call it), praying each speck that appeared on the horizon might be the ship that would rescue her.

There was a loud knock on the door. Hurriedly, Princess Pandora hid her telescope under her skirts.

'Come in,' she said irritably.

A tall dark figure entered the room.

'My dear Princess Pandora, allow me to introduce myself. My name is Count Nasty.'

Princess Pandora peered through her glasses at the Count as he bowed politely.

'What do you want?' she snapped.

'Your father, King Brian, asked me to come. It seems you tried to run away. I'm here to make sure that it doesn't happen again or indeed to make sure that a certain Princess Portia doesn't get into the palace,' said Count Nasty, evilly.

Pandora felt a moment of panic but tried not to show it.

'Just to let you know, there are guards at every corner and all of the guests are being checked at the main gate. There's no way she'll be able to get in and out and whisk you away,' Count Nasty said with a smirk.

'I don't know what you're talking about,' lied Princess Pandora. 'I haven't had anything to do with her since we were at school. I have no idea why she might come here!'

'Well then, if she *does* come you won't mind if I catch her, will you? She got away from me once before. She won't get away again.' Count Nasty sneered as he headed back towards the door.

'I'd heard it was twice,' murmured Pandora under her breath.

'What was that?' said Count Nasty as he turned and glared at Princess Pandora.

'Oh nothing!' replied Pandora, thinking fast. 'I just said ... erm ... she doesn't sound very nice!'

'Hmm,' he said suspiciously, 'Anyway, just remember, you're being watched.' And with a swirl of his cloak, Count Nasty left the room.

Princess Pandora went back to the window.

'Oh dear,' she said to herself as she looked out to sea, 'what if Portia does come and gets caught? Then we're both in big trouble!'

Chapter Three

The *Flying Pig* arrived at the harbour just as dusk was falling.

'We'll sail around to the next bay and drop anchor,' said Portia. 'Then Jim and I will take the rowing boat and go ashore.'

'What about me?' asked Peppermint. 'Can't

I come too?'

'No,' said Portia. 'I want you to stay in charge here. The ship will need to be ready to sail as soon as we return. Someone should keep watch from the crow's nest at all times, and if anything goes wrong you must sail without us. There's no point in all of us being captured.'

There were cries of disapproval from the crew at the thought of abandoning their captain.

'Pipe down, ladies! That's an order,' she roared.

'Aye, aye, Captain,' said Peppermint reluctantly. 'Good luck,' she added.

'I think we're going to need it,' said Portia, climbing down to the rowing boat.

Portia and Jim pushed themselves away from the ship and began to row to shore, Squawk perched in the boat next to Portia. The rest of their ship-mates watched them disappear into the night, all desperately hoping that they would return safely.

'We're going to have to play this one by ear, Jim,' said Portia as they pulled on the oars.

'It's going to be tricky enough getting into the palace, let alone rescuing Princess Pandora and getting her out again.'

Jim looked worried. 'I wonder if "you know who" has been looking for you.'

A shiver went down Portia's spine.

'Yes, I've been wondering the same thing,' replied Portia.

As they neared the shore, Portia and Jim tied the rowing boat to a mooring buoy and waded ashore.

'Stay in the shadows,' said Portia as they squelched their way up the wooden steps that led from the water's edge. They could hear the buzz of the coastal town above them.

When they reached the top of the steps, Portia gasped, the colour draining from her face.

'What is it, Captain?' said Jim, terrified.

Portia pointed.

On every building, lamp post and notice board was a wanted poster with her name on it!

Squawk ruffled his feathers nervously.

'I'm going to need a disguise,' said Portia as they crept behind a pile of lobster pots.

'I know! Follow me,' she whispered, picking up one of the lobster pots and carrying it on her shoulder to hide her face. They hurried away from the busy harbour into the dark back streets.

'Look!' said Jim. He pointed up to the washing lines which were strung across from the windows in the alleyway.

'Excellent! Well spotted, Jim,' exclaimed Portia. She put the lobster pots on top of each other and climbed up. She stretched up but still couldn't reach. 'Squawk! Fly up and un-peg some clothes for me.'

Squawk followed instructions and Portia quickly
switched her clothes.

'OK!' She said rolling up her own clothes,
'Now I don't look at all like a pirate. Let's go!'

They trudged up the hill towards the main
gates of the palace. There were lots of other
people making the same journey so they hid
themselves amongst the crowds.

Some were clearly wedding guests and, as they approached the Palace, Portia and Jim saw a queue of people having their invitations checked by a couple of burly soldiers before being allowed to enter.

'We'll never get in that way without an invitation,' said Portia, looking all around her. 'This wall goes right around the Palace. It's too high to climb and there are so many people around we'd be seen anyway. We'll have to find another way in.'

All of a sudden there was shouting and commotion as a scuffle broke out at the main gates.

'Round the back, you!' ordered one of the soldiers.
'I told you, guests only at the main gate!'

'HOW DARE YOU!' yelled a large fat man
with an Italian accent. 'I am Arnoldo Arnoldi the
famous Italian chef and you WILL let me in!'

'Round the back, I said!' shouted the soldier
giving the chef a shove. 'Servant's entrance!'

'Dis is a disgrace!' bellowed Arnoldi. 'I will
speak to the King about dis, you will see!' He
trooped off in a huge huff with his little army of
cooks and washer-uppers.

'Quick, Jim!' said Portia grabbing his arm and weaving her way through the crowd who had been watching the spectacle. 'This could be our way in!'

They followed the mob of cooks with their cart-loads of food and equipment until they reached the back entrance of the Palace. The guards at this gate were not being quite so careful as their colleagues at the main gates, so when the still red-faced and angry chef Arnoldi blustered his way through, it was easy enough for Portia and Jim to sneak through with them.

Squawk, who'd been watching what was going on, flew in through a window nearby and perched in the rafters of the kitchen.

'We're in!' whispered Portia to Jim.

'Yes, but now what?' He glanced around nervously.

'Now we have to look the part,' she said. 'I wonder where they keep the uniforms?'

'Look over there,' said Jim. At the other end of the huge kitchen, the catering staff had formed a queue. At the front, a friendly grey-haired lady was dishing out uniforms.

'Perfect!' smiled Portia, dragging Jim over to join the line.

'Here you are, dear,' said the grey-haired lady as she handed Portia a clean, white uniform.

'New, are we? I haven't seen you before.' She winked.

'Yes, Madam,' said Portia. 'Thank you.'

'And here's one for you,' said the lady, winking again at Jim.

'Thank you, Madam,' said Jim, taking his uniform and smiling sweetly.

As the lady turned to the next person in the line, Portia and Jim sneaked off to find a hiding place.

'In here!' said Portia, opening the door to a storeroom. 'We can change into our uniforms and

stay here till morning.' She waved at Squawk and
he flew down to join them.

As the three made themselves comfortable in
the storeroom, they heard angry voices coming
from the kitchen.

'Oi! Who's got my uniform? This one's too
small.'

'Yeah. Mine's too small n'all!' Said another voice.

Portia and Jim looked through a crack in the door and tried not to laugh out loud at what they saw. Two hairy kitchen hands were dressed in uniforms that were at least three sizes too small.

'Don't blame me,' said the grey-haired lady 'they're the last two left.'

'Oops, I suppose that's our fault!' giggled Portia as she settled down on a large sack of oats.

'I daresay it is!' answered Jim with a grin.

Chapter Four

The next morning, Portia awoke to the sounds and smells of breakfast being prepared.

'Mmmm. That smells goooooooood!' said Portia, breathing in deeply.

She shook Jim gently to wake him up. 'Jim, Jim, it's time to get up.'

'What?' Jim yawned. 'Mmmm. What's that delicious smell?' he said. His stomach rumbled agreement.

'They're making breakfast,' said Portia. 'We'd better get out of this cupboard and find a way to get to Princess Pandora.'

They brushed down their uniforms and Portia opened the door carefully.

The kitchen was a buzz of activity. As well as breakfast, food was being prepared for the wedding feast later in the day. Signor Arnoldi was already looking very hot and bothered, bellowing orders left, right and centre.

'You there,' He pointed at two kitchen hands. 'I needs zees vegetables prepared. Where are da chickens, they should be going into de oven already. Has anyone even started to maka da soup? Pronto, pronto everybody! Dis feast will not make itself!' Arnoldi wiped his sweaty brow. 'AND ze Princess's breakfast is ready, it needs to be taken to the tower, who is—'

Portia stepped forward quickly. 'We'll take it, sir,' she volunteered.

'Be quick about it then!' said Arnoldi waving his arms around like an octopus. 'And get right back down here and peel zees potatoes.'

'Yes, sir, of course, sir!' said Portia and Jim together.

They grabbed the breakfast trolley, smuggled Squawk and their own clothes quickly onto the shelf at the bottom and pushed it out of the kitchen, snatching themselves a couple of croissants as they went.

'Which way do we go?' Jim asked Portia, munching on his croissant.

'I think it must be . . . this way,' she replied, making a right turn down the passageway towards the stairs at the end and shoving a whole croissant in her mouth at once.

They lifted the trolley up the stairs and found themselves standing in a large hallway.

Everywhere was decorated in pink, blue and gold ribbon and the lady with grey hair was arranging flowers in vases that were all around the room. It looked quite beautiful. Portia and Jim began to push the trolley across the hall.

'Where are you going with that?' roared a guard, standing in front of the trolley to block their way.

'It's . . . er . . . the Princess's breakfast,' stuttered
Jim. Portia tried to hide her face in case she was
recognised.

'Don't you shout at them, you bully,' snapped
the nice grey-haired lady, stepping in between
them. 'They're new here. They just don't know
where to go.' She turned to Jim and Portia and
winked. 'It's through the door behind you and
straight up to the top, my dears. Mind your step
though, it's a bit steep.'

'Thank you, Madam!' said Jim, much relieved. The lady glowered at the guard who returned sheepishly to his post while Portia and Jim sped the trolley through the door, breathing a huge sigh of relief as it closed behind them.

'Why does she keep winking at us?' asked Jim.

'I dunno,' said Portia, puzzled. 'Maybe she's got a twitch.' She looked up at the winding stone staircase in front of them. 'It's quite a climb.'

Portia winced. 'Oh well, here goes.'

They puffed, panted and groaned their way to the top of the stairs and by the time they reached the top they were gasping for breath.

'Phew!' wheezed Portia. 'That was hard work!'

Jim couldn't even speak.

Looking down a short dark corridor they saw two guards standing outside a door.

'That's obviously where Princess Pandora is being kept,' Portia whispered to Jim as she began to push the trolley towards the door.

'Princess Pandora's breakfast is served!' Jim said brightly to the guards.

They looked down at the pair slightly suspiciously. Portia turned her head away in case they recognised her.

'Not seen you here before,' one of them said.

'Er no, we're new,' said Jim eagerly. 'Here to help with the lovely Royal Wedding.'

'OK,' said the other guard. 'Leave the trolley here. We'll take it in to the Princess. You can come back for it later.'

'Oh no,' Portia blurted out. 'I mean, we were told to wait and make sure Princess Pandora eats her breakfast and *then* take it back.'

'I suppose that's all right,' said the first guard. 'She *should* eat something this morning. All right then, go in but remember we're right outside.'

'Yes, sir. Right, sir. *Absolutely*, sir!' said Jim, like a real creep.

The door was unlocked and Portia pushed the trolley inside.

Chapter Five

Princess Pandora was sitting sulkily on her bed with her back to the door.

'You may as well take it away,' she snapped. 'I'm not going to eat anything.'

'Ooooh, good! Because we're starving, aren't we, Jim?' Portia said greedily.

Princess Pandora jumped up and turned around.

'PORTIA!' Pandora squealed running over to give her a hug.

'Shhhhhh!' said Portia. 'They'll hear!'

The door flew open and one of the guards burst in.

'What's going on in here?' he asked.

'Er, nothing.' Pandora blushed. 'I'm… just really pleased that my breakfast is here. Now leave my room immediately, I want to eat!'

'Sorry, your Highness,' said the guard uncomfortably, and closed the door.

They wheeled the trolley away from the door and sat down to share the breakfast. Squawk came out from under the cloth on the trolley and gobbled up the fruit.

'Thank you so much for coming,' said Pandora. 'I knew you wouldn't let me down!'

'Steady on,' said Portia. 'We're not out of here yet. We've got to find a way to get out of this room for a start.'

'Count Nasty's here, you know,' Pandora warned her. 'He's put posters up everywhere and the Palace is crawling with guards.'

'Yes, we know,' said Portia. 'If it hadn't been for that old grey-haired lady downstairs, we'd be in big trouble already.'

'That must've been Martha.' Pandora smiled. 'She has known me since I was a baby. I told her that I had asked you to come and save me. I knew she'd help if she could.'

'That explains the winking,' laughed Portia. Still munching a piece of toast and jam, she wandered around. 'What we need to do first, is find a way to get you out of this room.'

'If we could only get downstairs it would be a start. My workshop's down there, and all my tools. There's nothing up here that's of any help,' groaned Pandora.

Portia scratched her head.

'When we've finished stuffing our faces we'll have to take the trolley back downstairs to the kitchen. Wait a minute . . . that's it! The *trolley*!' Jim and Pandora both looked quizzically at Portia.

'We'll take you out on the trolley, the same way Squawk came in! The cloth will hide you if you squeeze on the shelf underneath!' She said excitedly.

'I'll never get on there in this puffball of a dress.' Said Pandora.

'That's no problem, you can change into my clothes, they're under there already. And we can leave your dress up here.'

'Won't the guards notice she's gone?' queried Jim.

'Ah no, you see that's why we leave the dress. We can stuff it with the pillows and prop it up in the chair,' explained Portia.

'That's brilliant! They're so stupid I'm sure they'd fall for it,' said Pandora. 'Let's do it!' Pandora changed into Portia's clothes while Portia and Jim set about making a reasonably convincing dummy out of the pillows and dress.

'What about the head?' asked Jim.

'Easy!' replied Portia. 'Where is the wedding veil?'

49

'Here,' said Pandora, passing it over.
Portia rolled a bed sheet up into a ball, balanced
it on top of the dress, then carefully draped the
veil over the top.

'There,' she said, stepping back. 'Nobody
would notice. It's facing out of the window, so
you'd have to come around the front to see
there's nobody inside. Squawk, meet us downstairs.
OK, Pandora. Let's take you for a ride!'

Chapter Six

Portia and Jim opened the door and pushed the trolley outside.

'Princess Pandora is trying on her wedding veil,' Portia said to the guards. 'She asked not to be disturbed.'

The guards glanced in the room.

'OK then. Back to the kitchens with you!'
They pushed the trolley, a little shakily, to the top
of the stairs.

'Grit your teeth, Jim,' said Portia. 'This is going
to be even worse than it was on the way up. We
mustn't let them see how heavy it is.'

Jim lifted the trolley and winced slightly. It was
very heavy. He saw the guards were still watching
so he forced a smile as they went down the
stairs. But the further they went, the more his
smile became a grimace.

As soon as they were out of the guards'
sight they stopped to get their breath back.

'One ... *puff* ... more ... *puff* ... flight to go,'
said Portia, her muscles aching, 'Pandora said her
room was on the first floor.'

'Thank goodness for that,' said Jim. 'I'm
exhausted!'

They stumbled down the last few steps and
weaved their way down the corridor to
Pandora's room.

'This is it!' whispered a voice from under the
trolley as they stopped outside the third door
along. Portia opened the door, pushed the trolley
into the room and she closed the door behind
her. Then she and Jim collapsed in a heap on the
floor. But they were not alone.

'You must be Portia the Pirate Princess!' said a little voice from the corner of the room.

Pandora climbed out from under the breakfast trolley.

'Sophie! What are you doing here?'

'Waiting for you, Sis,' said the girl who looked like a miniature version of Pandora. 'Martha told me that Princess Portia was here to help you escape and I want to come too.'

'This is my sister, Sophie,' Pandora said to Portia and Jim.

'Pandora's told me all about you!' said Sophie, grabbing Portia's hand and shaking it enthusiastically. 'Please, please take me with you, I want to join your crew and see the world. And if Pandora runs away they'll probably send me to Moronia instead and you'd have to rescue me anyway.'

'That may be true,' said Portia, rather flattered by Sophie's enthusiasm, 'but I don't know how any of us are going to get out of here yet.'

'It's a shame we can't all go out on trolleys,' Jim wheezed.

Portia and Pandora looked at each other.

'What if . . .' said Portia, scratching her head.

'Hmmm . . . yes,' replied Pandora, 'I think I've got an idea!' She ran over to her desk and took out paper and a pencil.

'Sophie, is your breakfast trolley still in your room?' Pandora asked.

'Yes, I think so.'

'Go and get it, quickly.' As Pandora started drawing, she called Portia over.

'Here, look at this. This is what I think we should do.'

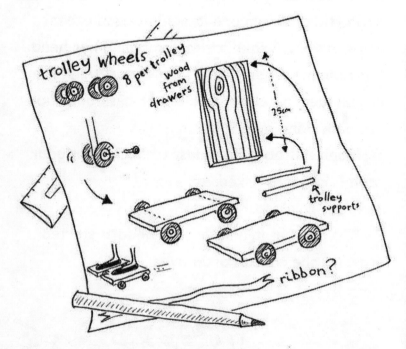

'If we have wheels on our shoes, we'll go too fast for anyone to catch us, especially when we get out of the Palace, it's all down hill!'

'You're a genius!' Portia exclaimed, giving her a hearty clap on the back. 'Let's get started, what do we need to do first?'

'Right,' said Pandora. 'Here's a screwdriver. You can start by unscrewing the wheels from the trolleys. Jim, empty one of the drawers in the wardrobe, we'll need the wood from the bottom.' They set to work.

Pandora packed two bags to take with them, one with a set of tools and another with her notebooks and Portia's coat.

When Sophie returned with her trolley, Portia unscrewed the other set of wheels.

'How are we going to get them to stay on our feet?' asked Portia.

'I was just coming to that. Sophie, run downstairs and grab some of the ribbon from the hall. Don't let anyone see you.'

'Righto! Back in a jiffy!' said Sophie.

While Sophie was downstairs, they sawed the

pieces of wood down to foot-sized lengths and screwed on the wheels.

'OK! We all need a pair each, so that's eight altogether,' said Pandora. 'Portia, can you drill some holes in the sides for the ribbons to go through?'

'Of course. We'd better hurry though. It won't be long until they come looking for you.' Portia said a little nervously. She finished drilling the holes just as Sophie returned with the ribbons. Sophie and Pandora threaded the ribbons through the holes and soon the wheeled shoes were ready.

'Who's going to try them first?' asked Pandora, holding up a pair of the shoes proudly.

'I will!' volunteered Portia grabbing them and tying them to her feet. 'Whoa!!' She stood up and tried to steady herself.

Carefully, Portia slid one foot in front of the other until she was propelling herself around the room. 'This is great fun! You guys have to have a try!'

They all tied on a pair of shoes and in a few minutes they were all rolling around the room,

bumping into furniture. They didn't all find it as easy as Portia did.

'Ow!' said Jim crashing into the wall for the third time and landing on his bottom. 'This is harder than it looks!'

'Keep practising, Jim! We'll have to leave in a minute,' said Portia, helping him up. 'Pandora, you'll have to take the lead until we get out of the Palace, Jim and I don't know the way. Squawk, go back to the ship and let them know we're on our way.'

'Aye, aye Cap'n,' squawked Squawk.

'OK. We'll go down the main staircase, the sides slope all the way down and we'll go *really* fast.' Portia put one of the bags on her back, replaced her captain's hat and headed towards the door.

'Right everyone,' she said. 'It's time to go!'

Chapter Seven

Sophie opened the door gingerly and stepped outside.

'Coast's clear!' she said to the others.

They bundled outside, Jim still having trouble staying on his feet.

'Ready, steady . . . GO!' said Portia and the race began.

'This way!' whispered Pandora as she sped towards the end of the corridor and around the corner. Sophie, Portia and Jim followed, Jim bouncing off the sides as he went, knocking over a plant pot and crashing into a suit of armour.

'Ooops!' he said feebly as it fell to the floor with an ear-splitting clank.

'That's torn it!' said Portia with her fingers in her ears.

'Sorry!' whimpered Jim. 'I'm doing my best.'

'I know,' she replied encouragingly. 'Don't worry, just keep going.'

'What was *that*?' a voice boomed from downstairs.

'Quick!' said Pandora. 'Stay with me, we're heading for the staircase.'

They all followed as Pandora jumped onto the side of the staircase and flew downstairs at what seemed like a hundred miles an hour.

'Wheeeeeee!!' shouted the three princesses as they hurtled down the stairs in a blur.

'Helllllllp!' yelled Jim following after them. 'I can't look!'

By now a small crowd had gathered in the downstairs hall. Portia spotted the sinister figure of Count Nasty running to secure the door.

'He's going for the door!' she shouted.

As they watched, the old grey-haired lady, Martha, stepped into the hall with a huge vase of flowers. She had spotted the Count too.

'Ooops-a-daisy!' Martha said as she accidentally on purpose poured the entire contents into Count Nasty's path. 'Silly me! Here, make sure you don't slip,' she said grabbing his arm tightly.

'Get off me you stupid woman, they're getting away!' roared Count Nasty as the three princesses followed by a terrified Jim sped past. 'Guards!' he bawled. 'Get to the main gate!'

They dashed through the streets as fast as their wheels would carry them. Jim was still out of control. Not only that, but he had his eyes half closed in fear and was still bumping into things.

'Ooops!' he said knocking over a vegetable stall, and 'Sorry!' as he sped away.

'Yeooow!' cried an old man hopping about after Jim ran over his toes.

'Sorry . . . sorry madam . . . oops . . . excuse me . . .' things were knocked flying all over the place as Jim tried to keep up with the speeding princesses in front of him. He left a trail of chaos behind him as they got closer and closer to the main gates.

'Oh no!' said Sophie as she glanced ahead.
'Look!' She pointed.

The drawbridge was being raised.

'Don't panic!' shouted Portia. 'Just go faster!
We can make it.'

They zoomed towards the drawbridge as it slowly began to lift. Behind them, they could hear the sound of galloping horses.

'It's Count Nasty!' Portia yelled. 'Keep going!' They bumped over the cobbles in front of the main gate and followed Portia as she gathered speed.

'Here goes!' whooped Portia as she approached the lifting drawbridge. The others followed although none of them were entirely convinced it was a good idea.

'Wheee!'

'Wheeee!'

'Wheeeee!'

'Arrrrrrrrrrrrrgh!'

They all yelled as they flew off the end of the
drawbridge and floated through the air.

Portia made an almost perfect landing on the other side followed by Pandora and Sophie whose landings were a little shakier. Jim, eyes tight shut, landed safely . . . upside down in a bush. Count Nasty, following on horseback, was left

looking over the fully raised drawbridge, shaking his fists.

'Whoo hoo! That was GREAT!' said Portia, looking around to see they were still all in one piece. 'Jim, are you OK?'

'Er . . . yes,' He said uncertainly, climbing out of the bush and pulling bits of twigs and leaves from his hair. He wobbled unsteadily towards her.

'OK! Pandora, Sophie, follow me and Jim back

to the harbour. They'll have the drawbridge back down any minute, so there's no time to waste.'

They pushed off and sped down the hill to the harbour, untied their wheeled shoes and climbed down the steps to the boat. By the time they had rowed back to the ship they could see a figure on horseback riding towards the harbour.

There was a huge cheer as the four of them

climbed on board the *Flying Pig*.

'Thank goodness you're back!' gushed Peppermint helping Portia onto the deck. 'Good to see you, Pandora!'

'Are we ready to sail, Bosun Betty?' asked Portia, running up to take the wheel as she changed back in to her Captain's clothes. Squawk flew over to take his usual place on her shoulder.

'Aye Captain!' said Betty giving the signal to weigh anchor.

'There'll be time for introductions later, everyone. Right now it's all hands on deck. Count Nasty is after us. His ship, the *Sea Serpent*, is one of the fastest on the high seas so if we've any hope of out-running her we must sail as if our lives depend on it. Stations everyone, it's time to get out of here!'

Chapter Eight

The *Flying Pig* surged through the water away from the harbour and towards the open sea.

Portia handed control of the wheel to the Second Mate Claire and took Pandora and Sophie to her cabin.

'Leave your tools here for now, we'll sort you out some sleeping quarters later.' She looked out of the window at a speck in the distance. 'I'll bet that's Count Nasty on our tail already but it's too far to tell right now.'

'Here, use this,' said Pandora handing Portia her telescope.

Portia held up the telescope and looked through.

'Wow! This is excellent,' she said. 'Yes, that's the *Sea Serpent* all right. It won't be that long before Count Nasty catches up. He's bound to try and board the ship.'

Jim and Peppermint entered the cabin.

'Emily's spotted a ship on the horizon. Donnatella's in a panic already,' said Jim. 'What shall we do?'

'Yes, it's definitely Count Nasty.' Portia scratched her head.

'Don't you have any cannons, Captain?' asked Sophie. 'You can't have a pirate ship without cannons.'

'Cannons yes, cannon balls no. Not much gunpowder either. We need something else. Something that we don't need gunpowder for.'

'That's my job then!' said Pandora. 'Show me what you've got that I can use.'

'Good idea! Peppermint, take Pandora round the ship, she can use anything that she thinks is helpful,' instructed Portia.

'But what can we use for ammunition?' asked Jim as Peppermint and Pandora headed out on deck.

Sophie piped up again. 'If you've got some nets you could drag some rocks up from the sea bed or something.'

'We haven't got any nets big enough for that ... although ... rocks ... Wait a minute, that's it!' Portia rushed to the door. 'Nancy! Nancy! Where are you?!'

'Here, Captain,' said Nancy, running from the main deck.

'Where are your rock cakes?' Portia asked.

'Well, they're not the best, Captain, they're a bit erm ... 'rocky' really, or at least the first three

batches were, then the next one was a bit gooey and ... but if you're hungry I could make you a nice sandwich?'

'Never mind all that!' Portia said impatiently. 'Are they still in the galley?'

'Yes, Captain, everybody said they weren't hungry,' said Nancy sadly.

'Excellent! Go down and bake as many as you can and make sure they're your rockiest mixture. Shipmates Donnatella and Anisha can help. Jim, go down and bring up on deck all the cakes you can find. We have our ammunition!'

Jim bundled Nancy out of the room before she could protest and they disappeared down to the galley. Almost at the same time, Pandora rushed in.

'I need paper and pencils,' she said. 'We're going to make a trebuchet!'

'A what?!' said Portia. 'What on earth is a trebuchet?'

Pandora began to draw.

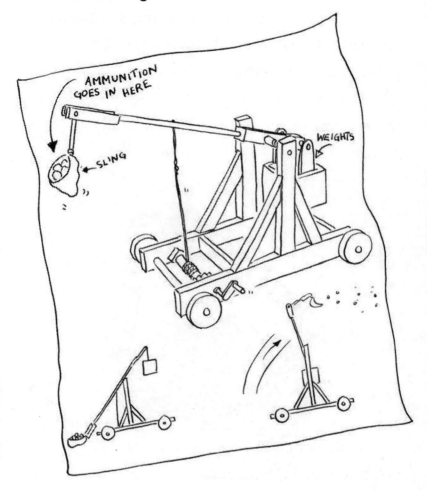

'It's a kind of giant catapult,' she said. 'Look. It's really simple but it can shoot things a long way. If you have anything to put in it that is . . .'

'Sorted!' said Portia as Jim came back with the first four batches of Nancy's special rock cakes. 'Let's get building.'

Chapter Nine

Portia, Jim and Sophie followed Pandora's instructions. They sawed, hammered, drilled, nailed and glued until the giant catapult was ready.

'Ship Ahoy!' Emily cried out from the crow's nest.

'Bosun Betty!' called Portia. 'How close is the *Sea Serpent* now?'

'She'll be on us in about fifteen minutes Cap'n, she's getting mighty close.'

'We need to make a turn soon so that we can catch her amidships. Let her get a bit closer and then steer us starboard,' ordered Portia.

'Aye aye, Cap'n!' said Betty.

'We'd better test this thing to see if it works.'

'It will, don't worry,' said Pandora. 'My inventions *always* work!' Sophie smiled proudly at her sister. 'Let's roll it on deck. We can try it out and make any final adjustments.'

Meanwhile, on board the *Sea Serpent*, Count Nasty smiled his evil smile.

'Shall we man the cannons, Sir?' asked the Chief Petty Officer.

'Of course not, you fool,' sneered Count Nasty. 'There are four Princesses on board. For goodness' sake, can you imagine what would happen if they were harmed? No, we'll just go alongside, board her and take her back to port. They've no weapons on board I'm sure. You're not frightened of a bunch of girls, are you?' he crowed.

'No, Sir. Of course not, Sir,' said the sailor, rather unconvincingly.

Count Nasty stared at the *Flying Pig* and sniffed the air. 'I'm sure I can smell cooking,' he said. 'Why would they be making cakes at a time like this?'

'I don't know, Sir. Owww!' said the Chief Petty Officer, as something very hard bounced off his head and into the sea.

'Bullseye!' roared Portia, on board the *Flying Pig*. 'I've said it before and I'll say it again, Pandora you're a genius!'

Pandora blushed.

'Prepare to come about!' ordered Bosun Betty.

The ship began to turn to starboard.

'Ready the cannons, Peppermint,' commanded Portia. 'It's nearly time for action!'

Each of the four cannons was loaded and primed, a basket of rock cakes placed next to each of them. The giant catapult stood in the middle of the deck, loaded with cakes and ready to fire. The *Flying Pig* turned until it was side on to the *Sea Serpent*. Portia raised her arm.

'Ready! Aim! Fire!'

Chapter Ten

A hail of solid rock cakes flew through the air
and landed on the crew of the *Sea Serpent.*

   'Oww!'

   'Oooof!!'

   'Ooooo!!!'

   'Ouch!!!'

'What the . . . ?' Count Nasty bent down and picked up one of the missiles. 'They're . . . firing . . . cakes!!' he shouted.

'They may be cakes,' said the Purser, 'but they are as hard as rocks!' He rubbed his shoulder.

'I've got a nose bleed!' said one of his ship-mates, pathetically.

'Oh no!' shouted someone else. 'Here come some more . . . everybody duck!'

There was another hail of rock cakes. Most of the crew hit the deck, the rest of them diving down the hatches.

'Be quiet, you feeble idiots!' said Count Nasty, stepping out from behind the main mast.

'On your feet and steer us alongside. They can't hurt you with cakes!!' As he spoke, one of the cakes caught him right in the face.

'Ouch!' he yelled angrily, rubbing his cheek.

He looked around at the cowering sailors. 'What are you waiting for,' Count Nasty bellowed 'I said *board that SHIP!*'

The crew crept out reluctantly from their hiding places and began to steer towards the *Flying Pig*.

'More cakes!' shouted Portia as the crew of the *Flying Pig* loaded and re-loaded the cannons and the giant catapult.

Squawk was helping to pass out the cakes and Twiggy was eating the crumbs.

'This is the last batch,' said Jim as he and Nancy stumbled up the stairs to the main deck. 'There's one more lot in the oven but apart from that there's only cake mixture.'

'They're trying to pull alongside, Captain!' said Betty.

'Keep loading those cannons!' Portia yelled. Pandora and Sophie released another catapult full of cakes at the crew of the *Sea Serpent*. Jim ran over to help them re-load.

'Try and keep our distance,' ordered Portia. 'We mustn't let them get too close.'

A grappling hook attached to a rope came flying across from the *Sea Serpent* and caught in the rigging of the *Flying Pig*. One of the *Sea Serpent's* crew grabbed the rope and began to edge along it. Portia grabbed a handful of cakes. She threw one at the sailor on the rope.

'Take that!' shouted Portia.

'Ow!' moaned the sailor and lost grip with one hand.

'And that!' She threw another cake. It was a direct hit and the sailor let go of the rope and fell 'plop' into the sea.

Two more ropes flew across and landed on the deck.

'Quick,' said Portia, 'cut those ropes.'

'We're running out of cakes!' called Peppermint.

'So are we,' said Pandora. 'There's only enough left for one more load.'

'This is the last batch that Jim brought up from the galley. Hand them out, we'd better make them count. We haven't got time to bake any more.'

'They're a bit squidgy!' said Sophie as she began to load the catapult.

'They're all we've got! Just put them in,' said Portia, urgently. She picked up a couple herself and the warm cakes squashed in her hands. She hurled them at the *Sea Serpent*.

One of the cakes hit the head of the Chief Petty Officer, but instead of bouncing off, it just stuck in his hair. 'Oh dear,' thought Portia.

At the same time, Pandora let go the cakes from the giant catapult and they too just stuck where they landed. The pirate princesses watched as the crew of the *Sea Serpent* pulled the sticky cakes off their clothes and hair.

Portia smiled and called Jim over.

'How much mixture is there left?' she asked him.

'A couple of barrels I'd guess,' answered Jim.

'Great! Go down and get them, and bring Nancy with you. We need all hands on deck ... Oh yes, and tell them to bring some bowls.'

The sailors on the *Sea Serpent* had started throwing back some of the unbroken cakes and it was beginning to turn into a massive food fight. Squawk was dive bombing the *Sea Serpent* with some of the remaining cakes, trying hard not to get them stuck on his beak. Twiggy was still licking up the mess.

Jim, Peppermint and Nancy returned to the main deck, dragging the barrels of rock cake mixture.

'What do you want us to do with this?' asked Jim as he ran over to Portia.

'OK! Nancy, hand out the bowls. Everyone load up with the mixture, and hurry, they're getting too close for comfort.'

Indeed they were, and the sailor who'd fallen in the sea was climbing over the side of the *Flying Pig*. Sophie ran over and poured a bowlful of mixture on his head and pushed him back into the sea.

Pandora and Peppermint had filled the catapult with four bowls of cake mixture.

'Fire!' They yelled in chorus and let go the load.

Everyone watched as the cake mix flew through the air and landed 'splat!' in the rigging of the *Sea Serpent*. It began to drip through like a sieve and land on the sailors underneath.

'Yeuch! What is this stuff?' said a voice from the *Sea Serpent*.

'What's this disgusting gloop?' asked another.

The cannons on the *Flying Pig* began to fire once
more.

'Splot!'

'Splurge!'

'Splunge!'

'Splat!'

'Spludge!'

Globules of rock
cake mixture
landed on various
members of the
Sea Serpent's
crew.

There was an explosion of laughter on board the *Flying Pig* as they watched Count Nasty's crew stumbling around with cake mixture all over them. It had made the deck really slippery and they were finding it hard to stay on their feet. It was a hilarious sight.

'It looks like they've been attacked by a flock of giant seagulls!' shrieked Portia.

Jim was almost crying with laughter. 'I've . . . never . . . seen . . . anything . . . so   funny . . . in my whole life!'

Portia looked over to see Count Nasty, who had so far managed to avoid the sticky mess, trying to get the ship back on course. She ran over to one of the cannons and poured in another bowl of cake mix.

'Take aim! Fire!' she half shouted, half laughed as she fired the cannon. A large glob flew through the air and caught Count Nasty smack in the face!

Portia and her crew rolled around on deck laughing uncontrollably, even Squawk and Twiggy were hysterical.

'Captain . . .' said Jim, trying to pull himself together. 'We're almost out of mixture . . . we can't outrun the *Sea Serpent*, what are we going to do now?'

Portia quickly regained her composure.

'You're right, Jim,' she said, suppressing a final giggle, 'we're still in big trouble.'

Just as the words came out of Portia's mouth, Peppermint stumbled towards them.

'Captain, Captain! Is it my imagination, or can you smell burning?!'

They all stopped and sniffed and when they looked round they could see that smoke was billowing up from below decks.

'Oh NO!' screeched Nancy, running down towards the galley. 'My cakes!' She had got so involved in the battle that she'd forgotten there were still cakes in the oven.

Portia smiled a knowing smile.

'Clean out the cannons, shipmates. I know how we can finish them off!'

Chapter Eleven

Portia ran to the galley after Nancy.

'Follow me!' she said to Peppermint and
Pandora. 'Quick! Get the oven gloves.'

They poured the smoking, smouldering cakes
into a large metal cauldron.

'We mustn't let them cool down!' she said.
'We must get them back on as fast as we can.
Pandora, bring the serving tongs.'

When they got back on deck Portia looked
over at the *Sea Serpent*. The crew was beginning
to get back in control and making another
attempt to pull alongside.

Count Nasty had wiped the mess from his
face and was standing on the forecastle watching
them through his telescope.

'Ah ha!' he said, triumphantly, 'It looks like they're out of ammunition. Now we can take their ship! Prepare the grappling hooks! Prepare to board!'

Sophie was waiting for Portia and the others by the giant catapult.

'The cannons are cleared as you asked, Captain,' she said, 'but I thought we were out of ammunition.'

'Just watch!' said Portia. She ran along the line of cannons dropping in the smouldering cakes as she went. She poured the rest of them in the giant catapult.

'OK! Aim for the sails everyone! Ready! FIRE!' Portia ordered for the last time.

The air filled with smoking missiles. Some were still smouldering and as they hit the air they burst into flames. They flew through the air like tiny fireworks and peppered the sails of the *Sea Serpent*.

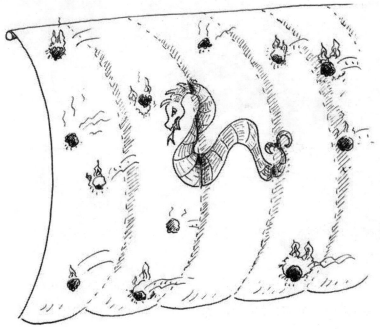

Lots of little holes began to appear in the sails and as both crews watched, the holes joined together and the sails started to burn. Count Nasty no longer looked quite so triumphant.

'Fire! FIRE!!' he shouted running up and down the ship. 'Man the pumps! Batten down the hatches!

Lower the lifeboats ...ABANDON SHIP!'

The entire crew of the *Sea Serpent* instantly
jumped into the water.

As the sails burned, the cake mixture that was stuck to them began to cook and the smell of baking wafted across the sea.

'Mmm. That batch of mixture smells rather nice!' said Portia.

Chapter Twelve

As the *Flying Pig* sailed further and further away
from the *Sea Serpent*, they watched the crew
climbing back on board. They could hear Count
Nasty ranting and raving as the sailors put out
the last of the fire with buckets of sea water.

'Fire's out, Captain,' said Emily from the crow's
nest.

'Good! After all we don't want them to burn
to a cinder.'

'But won't they follow us now?' said
Peppermint, slightly worried.

'I don't think they're going anywhere with sails like that,' Portia assured her. 'I think we're safe for the time being.'

Portia watched the *Sea Serpent* grow smaller and smaller in Pandora's telescope as the *Flying Pig* sailed over the horizon.

'I think we should celebrate,' said Portia to her crew. 'Let's have a welcome party for Pandora and Sophie.'

Nancy appeared on deck with a huge plate of perfectly cooked rock cakes.

They smelled delicious.

'You'll be needing these then,' she said proudly, 'I think I've got them right at last.'

'Excellent, Nancy!' said Portia. 'Tuck in, everyone!'

King Percy and Queen Doreen
are pleased to invite you to the wedding
of their dear daughter

Princess Pancake
to
Arctic Prince Ivor

at his Ice Palace in the Arctic circle
(please remember to bring your
thermal underwear)